Library of Congress Cataloging in Publication Data
Lloyd, David 1945-   Grandma and the pirate.
Summary: At the beach a little boy pretends to be
a pirate until his grandmother neatly turns the tables.
[1. Play—Fiction. 2. Grandmothers—Fiction.
3. Beaches—Fiction. 4. Pirates—Fiction] I. Tomblin,
Gill, ill, II. Title.
PZ7.L774Gr 1986   [E]   85-17054
ISBN 0-517-56023-2
10 9 8 7 6 5 4 3 2 1
First American Edition

Grandma and the Pirate

Written by
David Lloyd

Illustrated by
Gill Tomblin

Crown Publishers, Inc., New York

Hello.

My name is Robert.

Today I went to the
beach with Grandma.

We waded.

We played ball.

We caught a crab.

Grandma went to sleep.

I made a castle.

I made a boat.

I was a pirate.

When Grandma woke up,
she was my prisoner.

I made her walk
backward to the sea.

Then she made me walk
backward to the car
and we went home.